IMPOSSIBLE, POSSUM

by Ellen Conford

Illustrated by Rosemary Wells

LITTLE, BROWN AND COMPANY
Boston   Toronto

To David and Michael

RANDOLPH was a young possum. His mother worried about him.

"I don't understand it," she said. "All possums hang by their tails and sleep upside down. Why can't you?"

"I don't know," Randolph said glumly. "I certainly try hard enough."

"Try again," urged his father. "Maybe you just need more practice."

"All right," sighed Randolph. He edged out onto a limb of their tree. He held on tightly and took a deep breath.

"Don't look down," said his father.

"Don't be nervous," said his mother.

"You can do it!" called his brother.

"No, he can't," said his sister.

Randolph curled his tail around the branch, took another deep breath, and let go with his paws. He swung backwards and hung by his tail.

"Good for you!" shouted his father.

"My boy's growing up," sighed his mother.

"You're doing it!" cheered his brother.

"No, he's not," said his sister, as Randolph's tail uncurled and he fell to the ground, head first.

"Oh, my goodness!" said his mother. They all rushed to help Randolph.

"Are you hurt?" asked his mother anxiously.

"No more than usual," sighed Randolph. "I don't think I broke any bones."

His father shook his head.

"I just don't understand it. Your mother and I can hang by our tails; your brother Eugene can hang by his tail; your sister Geraldine can hang by *her* tail. It's the most natural thing in the world to sleep upside down."

To show Randolph how easy it was, Geraldine went back up the tree. She scurried out onto a limb, hung upside down, and sang "Pop, Goes the Weasel!" as she swung by her tail.

"Would you like to hear 'Mary Had a Little Lamb'?" she asked.

"Nobody likes a show-off," sulked Randolph.

"Why don't you try it again?" his father said. "You almost had it that time."

"It's impossible," Randolph said. "I just can't do it."

"Are you really trying your best?" asked his mother.

"If at first you don't succeed, try, try again," said his father.

"Practice makes perfect," added his brother.

His sister didn't say anything, because she was busy juggling three acorns while she hung by her tail.

"It's just impossible," Randolph sighed. "You might as well get used to it—I'm a failure."

"No, you're not," said his mother. "You just have to keep trying."

"I *can't* keep trying!" wailed Randolph. "Every time I try, I fall on my head. I get the most awful headaches."

"If you didn't hurt your head all the time, would you keep trying?" asked Eugene.

"I suppose so," said Randolph. "But how could I keep from hurting my head?"

"We could put a big pile of leaves under the tree," Eugene suggested, "so if you fall, you'll fall on something soft."

"*If* he falls! You mean, *when* he falls," sneered Geraldine.

"Never mind, Geraldine," said her father. "It's a very good idea. Now, go help your brothers collect some leaves."

Randolph, Eugene and Geraldine ran around gathering up leaves until there was a big pile of them beneath the branch where Randolph practiced.

"Here I go again," said Randolph. He climbed up the tree and out onto the branch, curled his tail over the limb, and hung upside down. His tail uncurled, and he fell head first into the pile of leaves.

"Do the leaves help?" asked his mother anxiously.

"A little," said Randolph, and climbed up the tree once more.

Again and again he tried to hang by his tail, and again and again he fell onto the pile of leaves.

His brother and sister went off to play. His

mother went in to prepare dinner. His father went for a walk.

Randolph kept hanging and falling.

Finally, he gave up.

"I have fallen for the last time," he said to himself, as he lay on his back in the middle of the pile of leaves.

"Maybe other possums can sleep upside down, but I am different. When my family goes to sleep and they all hang upside down on the branch, I will sleep on my pile of leaves. It's really very comfortable down here. As a matter of fact, it's so comfortable, I think I'll go to sleep right now." And he did.

Randolph woke to find that Geraldine and Eugene were jumping into his pile of leaves.

"Whee!" squealed Geraldine, "this is fun!"

"It may be fun for you," Randolph said gloomily. "For me, it's just a place to sleep."

He stood up and dusted himself off. A few leaves stuck to his tail.

"I'll help you," said Eugene. He tried to brush the leaves off Randolph's tail, but they wouldn't come off.

"They're stuck on," he said.

"Don't be silly," said Geraldine. "How can they be stuck?" She reached down and yanked a leaf off Randolph's tail.

"Ouch!" said Randolph. "That hurts!"

"Look!" Geraldine said. She pointed to a very small branch halfway up the tree. Something was slowly dripping from its end.

"Sap!" said Eugene. "You got sap on your tail and it made the leaves stick!"

Randolph stopped plucking leaves from his tail.

"Why didn't I think of this before?" he cried as he held his tail under the branch.

"If sap makes leaves stick to my tail," Randolph shouted as he scampered up the tree, "maybe it will make my tail stick to the branch."

18

Randolph wrapped his tail around the branch and held on with his paws until he was sure the sap was sticking. Then he let go and hung down. He didn't fall.

"Look at me!" he shouted. "Look, everybody!"

Eugene began clapping. His mother came outside and began to cry. His father heard the noise and came running.

"He's doing it!" Eugene squeaked. "Randolph's hanging by his tail!"

"Congratulations, Randolph," said his father. "You see, practice does make perfect."

"I don't think it was the practice so much as the sap," Randolph said.

"Sap?" said his father.

"Oh, my," said his mother.

"I think it's very clever," said Eugene.

"I think it's cheating," said Geraldine. "Anyway, how are you going to get down?"

"I never thought of that," Randolph admitted.

"Don't worry," his mother said kindly. "We'll just unwind your tail for you when you want to come down."

"Well, I think I'll just hang here for a while," said Randolph. "The world looks so different upside down. The sky is on the ground and the grass is up in the sky; it's very relaxing. I might even take a little nap."

He closed his eyes and fell asleep.

From then on, Randolph held his tail under the sap before the possums went to sleep, and his mother would unwind it for him when he woke up.

But one day, Randolph noticed that the sap had dried up.

"What will I do now?" he cried.

"Maybe you ought to try it again without the sap," suggested his father.

"It's impossible," said Randolph. "I always fall on my head."

"Randolph," reasoned his father, "winter is coming. In the winter, sap dries up. You must try to hang like the rest of us."

"Maybe we can find another tree with the sap coming out," said Eugene, who didn't always listen to his father. "I'll help you look."

So Randolph and Eugene went off together to look for a new supply of sap, and their father looked resigned.

"It's impossible," said Randolph, after they had been searching for some time. "I guess Father was right."

Sadly, Randolph and Eugene trudged back home.

"I might as well start making another pile of leaves," sighed Randolph. "I'll need a place to sleep."

Just then, Geraldine came scampering toward them.

"Look what I found!" she called. She showed Randolph two damp leaves.

"I found some sap, and I put it on these leaves," she said with a gleam in her eye. "Would you like me to rub them on your tail?"

"That's very nice of you, Geraldine," said Randolph, and he held out his tail.

Then he ran up the tree.

"I hope you put enough on," he worried.

"Oh, I did," said Geraldine cheerfully.

His mother and father came out when they heard his voice.

"Geraldine found some sap for me," Randolph said.

"What a good sister!" said her mother.

"It was nothing," said Geraldine modestly.

"Look!" called Randolph, who was hanging by his tail. "It works perfectly. Thank you, Geraldine."

Suddenly Geraldine shrieked, "Randolph, you're doing it! Look at Randolph! He's doing it!"

"Of course he's doing it," said Eugene. "He can always do it with the sap on his tail."

"No, no, no!" cried Geraldine, hopping up and down. "It wasn't sap, it was water! I put water on the leaves. It was a trick!"

"Water!" cried Randolph.

"What?" said his father.

"Oh, my," said his mother.

"That was a dirty trick," said Eugene.

"But he *is* hanging by his tail!" Geraldine persisted. "By *himself!*"

"I am?" gasped Randolph.

"He is!" said his father. "I'm amazed."

"Oh, Randolph, I'm so proud of you!" said his mother, and she was so happy she began to cry.

"I *can* do it! I can *do* it!" Randolph yelled.

"All you needed was a little confidence," said his father.

"And a tricky sister," said Eugene.

"You mean, a smart sister," said Geraldine.

The possums were so excited that they ran
out onto the branch and sang "For He's a
Jolly Good Fellow" to Randolph, as he hung
upside down by his tail.

And no one sang louder than Randolph.